FAITH RINGGOLD

HARLEM RENAISSANCE PARTY

Amistad

An Imprint of HarperCollinsPublishers

Dedicated to all the people I knew
growing up in Harlem in the 1930s

Poem on page 22: "Laughers" by Langston Hughes,
first published as "My People" in the June 1922 issue of *The Crisis*

Amistad is an imprint of HarperCollins Publishers.

Harlem Renaissance Party
Copyright © 2015 by Faith Ringgold
All rights reserved. Manufactured in China.
No part of this book may be used or reproduced in any manner whatsoever without written permission except
in the case of brief quotations embodied in critical articles and reviews. For information address HarperCollins
Children's Books, a division of HarperCollins Publishers, 195 Broadway, New York, NY 10007.
www.harpercollinschildrens.com

ISBN 978-0-06-057911-1 (trade bdg.) — ISBN 978-0-06-057912-8 (lib. bdg.)

The artist used acrylic paint on canvas paper to create the illustrations for this book.
Designed by Stephanie Bart-Horvath
14 15 16 17 18 SCP 10 9 8 7 6 5 4 3 2 1
❖
First Edition

Come one! Come all! in Harlem. Celebrate women of the Harlem everywhere

To a party today the great men and Renaissance. Everyone is invited!

It all began with a great big message written across the sky.

"Oh, can we go, Uncle Bates?" I pleaded.

"Now who can resist a party invitation written in the sky?" said Uncle Bates. "C'mon, Lonnie. We have a plane to catch."

People from all over the world were rushing to get tickets to Harlem.
"Will my favorite poet, Langston Hughes, be there?"
"It wouldn't be a party, Lonnie, without Langston," said Uncle Bates.

As soon as our plane took off, Uncle Bates got to talking with that proud look on his face. "Lonnie," he said, "we'll see musicians, poets, novelists, painters, activists, philosophers, and scholars: wise men and women, giants standing tall above the crowd, sharing dreams of a better life for all black people."

In no time, we were walking on Seventh Avenue with the giants of the Harlem Renaissance.

Just like Uncle Bates said, I could hear the drumbeats of a parade blocks away. "Uncle Bates!" I cried.

"I know, Lonnie," he said, "a parade is coming, but let's eat breakfast first. Well's Restaurant has the best fried chicken and waffles this side of heaven. We're meeting my friend Jack here."

"Hi, Jack," called Uncle Bates. "Meet my nephew, Lonnie.
Tell him how it feels to be Jack Johnson, the first black
heavyweight boxing champion of the world."

"It feels great, Lonnie, as great as eating fried chicken
and waffles smothered with hot buttered syrup. Dig in.
After we eat, we'll look for Langston, your favorite poet."

Mmm . . . mmm! Breakfast was so good. While we ate, all kinds of people (and giants, too!) came by to say hello to the champ and to meet Uncle Bates and me. Being with the champ made me feel like I was a champ, too.

We stepped outside just in time to catch the Marcus Garvey parade. The great leader looked like an African king, all dressed in purple with gold tassels and braids on his jacket. Everyone was cheering wildly and waving Garvey flags.

But when Marcus Garvey began to speak you could hear a pin drop. "I stand before you a proud black man, honored to be a black man, who would be nothing else in God's creation but a black man. I want you to feel the same way. . . ." The crowd roared. The celebration was on.

Uncle Bates said, "W.E.B. Du Bois at *The Crisis* magazine will know where we can find Langston."

"There's not much Dr. Du Bois doesn't know," said Jack. "He was the first black person to get a doctorate from Harvard, and he was a founder of the NAACP. If brains could box he'd be the champ." Jack danced around, throwing a few punches in the air.

"W.E.B.," said Jack, "my friend Lonnie wants to be a writer like you and Langston."

"I want to be creative like the writers and artists during the Harlem Renaissance," I said.

"Yes," said Dr. Du Bois. "We black folk had a new desire to create as though we had just awakened from a deep, deep sleep."

"Is that why we call it the Harlem Renaissance?" I asked.

"That is it exactly," said Dr. Du Bois. "Now go find Langston."

"Maybe he is at the Africana Art Gallery," said Dr. Du Bois. "Let's go see what they are showing."

On the walls, we saw paintings by William H. Johnson and Meta Vaux Warrick Fuller. Henry O. Tanner and Aaron Douglas had pictures. Sculptures by May Jackson, Augusta Savage, and Richmond Barthé were on pedestals.

Augusta Savage

Henry O. Tanner

"It is more exciting to see art in real life than in books,"
I said.

"Your aunt Connie taught me that this art shows the true
beauty of black people. It is as if we were invisible before
these artists painted us black," said Uncle Bates.

Aaron
Douglas

Africana
Art Gallery

Madam C. J. Walker's beauty school wasn't far from the gallery.

"Madam Walker invented a secret preparation for hair straightening and became America's first self-made female millionaire," said Uncle Bates. "She had a thirty-four-room mansion built just for her, and a beautiful apartment in Harlem. She gave lots of money to black colleges and other worthy causes."

Madam Walker waved to us from her convertible.

Before long, we were in front of the Harlem Opera House. I walked up to Paul Robeson. "Mr. Robeson, you are a great singer, actor, and athlete. How does it feel to be so famous that everybody knows your name?" I asked.

"I just want to be a tribute to my people and give boys like you, Lonnie, a chance to grow up to be strong men," said Mr. Robeson. Everyone applauded as if he had just sung a song.

"Here come two ladies, pretty as can be," said Jack.

"Hello! I just met you at Well's Restaurant," I said. "Miss Florence Mills, you played on Broadway in *Shuffle Along*. And you, Miss Jo Baker, went to Paris to become a star. The Harlem Renaissance didn't just stay in Harlem."

"No, Lonnie," said Uncle Bates. "The Harlem Renaissance went wherever the giants took it."

The ladies told us we could catch Langston at the Schomburg Library.

ZORA NEALE HURSTON
Schomburg Library

Zora Neale Hurston had just finished reading a story from *Mules and Men*, her collection of Negro folktales. The crowd roared with laughter.

Then I heard a soft voice repeating the words: "My people. My people." It was Langston Hughes, reading my favorite poem. I whispered along.

"My people. Dream-singers, story-tellers, dancers, loud laughers in the hands of Fate . . ."

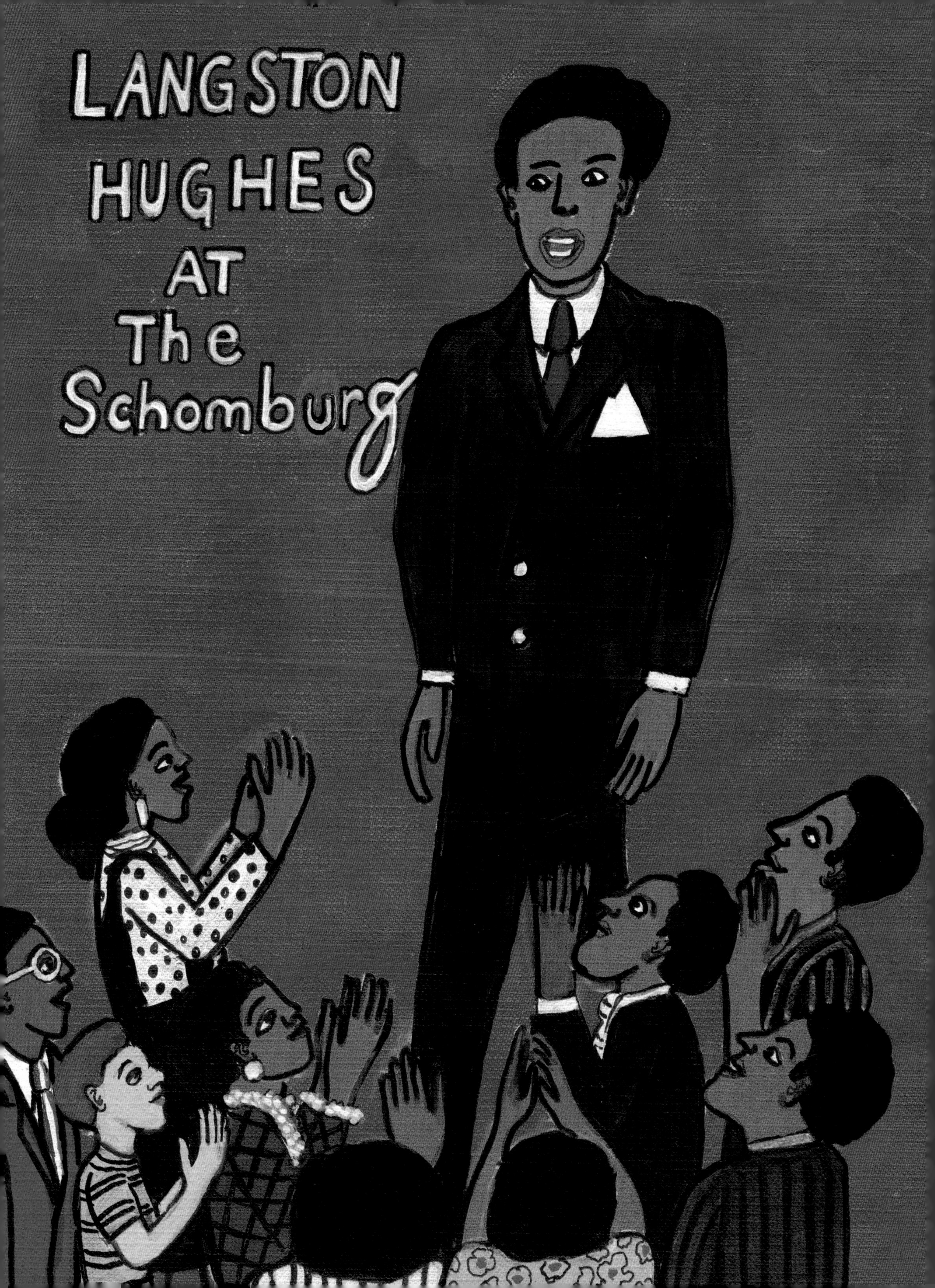
LANGSTON
HUGHES
AT
The
Schomburg

When I finally had a chance to talk to Mr. Hughes, I almost forgot what I was going to say.

"My name is Lonnie, Mr. Hughes, and I would like to know where you get the ideas for your poems."

"I get my ideas from jazz and the blues. I get my ideas from my people," said Mr. Hughes. "Do you write, Mr. Lonnie?"

"Yes, I guess so," I said.

"Then you are a writer," said Mr. Hughes.

I went away feeling like a giant.

Carter G. Woodson and Alain Locke were in the audience, too.

"Mr. Woodson," I said, "you started Negro History Week. Now it is Black History Month. I want to thank you for that."

"You are quite welcome, Lonnie," said Mr. Woodson.

"And Mr. Locke, you collect beautiful African masks. I have only seen them in books. I wish the kids at school could meet all my new friends," said Lonnie.

"I can't wait to tell Aunt Connie how proud you have made me today," said Uncle Bates. "You are the littlest giant of the Harlem Renaissance."

On the street, people were rushing into the Savoy Ballroom. "C'mon, you all. I feel like dancing. Let's show Lonnie how to cut a rug," said Uncle Bates.

A man in tattered clothes said, "Not everybody is dressed up, but everybody is welcome just as long as they can dance."

Someone said, "Say that again, man!" And everybody hummed, "Uh-huh."

Miss Mills and Miss Baker were the first ones on the dance floor.
"C'mon, little Lonnie! Let us grown folks show you how to do
the Charleston and the fox-trot."

The party was really getting hot. Fletcher Henderson's band was playing "Tuxedo Junction." Louis "Satchmo" Armstrong was on the trumpet, and Coleman Hawkins was on the saxophone. All the giants were dancing up a storm. We danced and danced till I got sleepy.

"Time to go home, Lonnie," said Uncle Bates.

"Can we do this again?" I asked.

"Lonnie, a party like this happens only once in a lifetime, but you will always remember meeting the giants," said Uncle Bates.

I hugged all my new friends.

"Keep dancing," they said.

Langston Hughes said, "Don't ever forget you're a writer, Mr. Lonnie."

We headed for home but the party was still going strong in Harlem.
"Uncle Bates, now I know why the Harlem Renaissance is so important."
"Why, Lonnie?"
"Because black people didn't come to America to be free. We fought for our freedom by creating art, music, literature, and dance."

"Now everywhere you look you find a piece of our freedom," Uncle Bates said.

"Like Marcus Garvey, I am so proud to be black. One day, I will be a famous writer just like Langston Hughes. You see, Uncle Bates," I said, "I learned from the giants of the Harlem Renaissance."

That night I had a dream that I was still at the Harlem Renaissance party, only I was a famous writer at my very own poetry reading.

Langston Hughes and all the artists and writers were there.
Alain Locke brought an African mask. Aunt Connie and Uncle
Bates were there with Jack Johnson. I was the proudest,
littlest giant of the Harlem Renaissance.

HARLEM RENAISSANCE GLOSSARY

LOUIS "SATCHMO" ARMSTRONG, also known as Pops, was an extraordinary musician born in New Orleans in 1901. When he moved to Harlem in 1924, he joined Fletcher Henderson's orchestra as a trumpeter. He later formed his own band, Louis Armstrong and His Hot Five. Today Satchmo is recognized as a cultural icon and artist who has had a lasting influence on jazz.

JOSEPHINE BAKER, an international star, singer, and dancer, was born in St. Louis, Missouri, in 1906. During the Harlem Renaissance she headed to New York City and performed in *Shuffle Along*, before moving to Paris to become one of Europe's most popular entertainers.

RICHMOND BARTHÉ, an African American modern sculptor, was born in Bay St. Louis, Mississippi, in 1901. After his graduation from the School of the Art Institute of Chicago, he moved to New York, where he built his career as an artist and won many awards.

BLACK HISTORY MONTH, which originally began as Negro History Week, was founded by Dr. Carter G. Woodson in 1926. It is an annual observance during the month of February that celebrates achievements by African Americans.

The **CHARLESTON** is a dance that originated in the 1920s in the African American community of a small island off the coast of Charleston, South Carolina. This jazz dance soon became very popular throughout the United States.

THE CRISIS magazine, founded in 1910 by W.E.B. Du Bois, is the official magazine of the National Association for the Advancement of Colored People (NAACP). *The Crisis* focuses on race and social injustice in the United States. *The Crisis* has published the works of many Harlem Renaissance writers.

AARON DOUGLAS, an African American painter and graphic artist also known as the Father of African American Art, was born in Topeka, Kansas, in 1899. His work includes portraits, murals, landscapes, and illustrations in anthologies and the magazines *The Crisis* and *Opportunity*.

W.E.B. DU BOIS was a historian, activist, author, and editor. He was born on February 23, 1868, in Great Barrington, Massachusetts, and attended Fisk

University. He also attended Harvard University, where he was the first African American to earn a doctoral degree. Dr. Du Bois was best known for his role as an intellectual activist who worked tirelessly for African American rights.

The FOX-TROT is a dance performed to ragtime music and believed to be named for Harry Fox, who popularized it in the early 1900s.

META VAUX WARRICK FULLER, an acclaimed sculptor, was born in Philadelphia in 1877. Fuller drew inspiration from songs of African Americans and African folktales for her sculptures. She is considered a forerunner to the Harlem Renaissance and is known for being one of the first artists to depict African American experiences in her work.

MARCUS GARVEY, born on August 17, 1887, in Jamaica, was a political leader, publisher, and journalist. He traveled to the United States in 1916 and organized the Universal Negro Improvement Association to promote social, political, and economic freedom for black people and to improve the conditions of people of African ancestry.

HARLEM is a large community in northern Manhattan in New York City. In the 1920s, an important African American artistic and literary movement known as the Harlem Renaissance began there.

The HARLEM OPERA HOUSE, once located on 125th Street between Seventh and Eighth Avenues in Harlem, opened in 1889. Designed by architect John B. McElfatrick, the Harlem Opera House was originally opened by businessman and composer Oscar Hammerstein and then later taken over by Frank Schiffman, who also owned the Apollo Theater.

The HARLEM RENAISSANCE was an African American artistic, literary, and cultural movement that took place in the 1920s through the 1930s. Originally known as the New Negro Movement, it was later changed to the Harlem Renaissance.

COLEMAN HAWKINS, a well-known tenor saxophone virtuoso, was born in St. Joseph, Missouri, in 1904. He played with Fletcher Henderson's orchestra during the Harlem Renaissance.

FLETCHER HENDERSON, a pianist and composer, was born in Cuthbert, Georgia, in 1897. After graduating from Atlanta University, he moved to New York City in 1920 hoping to find work as a chemist. Instead he became a bandleader who was at the forefront of the jazz music scene in Harlem in the 1920s.

LANGSTON HUGHES was a poet, activist, novelist, and playwright born in Joplin, Missouri, on February 1, 1902. His short stories, plays, and poetry from the

1920s through the 1960s presented colorful portrayals of black life in America. He was one of the foremost literary leaders of the Harlem Renaissance.

ZORA NEALE HURSTON, anthropologist, folklorist, and author, was also a literary star during the Harlem Renaissance. She was born in Notasulga, Alabama, on January 7, 1891. She is best known for her book *Their Eyes Were Watching God*, which was published in 1937.

MAY JACKSON, a sculptor born in 1877, studied art at the Pennsylvania Academy of Fine Arts, where she was the first African American to receive a scholarship. Jackson is best known for her sculptures of prominent people, such as W.E.B. Du Bois.

JAZZ is a style of music that originated in African American communities from New Orleans to St. Louis and beyond. It became especially popular in Harlem in the 1920s.

JACK JOHNSON, a heavyweight boxer, was born in 1878. In 1908, he became the first African American heavyweight boxing champion of the world. Johnson held on to his title until 1915.

WILLIAM H. JOHNSON, a renowned African American artist, was born in Florence, South Carolina, in 1901. He moved to New York City at the age of seventeen and studied at the National Academy of Design and later in Europe and North Africa. His work focused on the everyday life of African Americans.

ALAIN LOCKE was an American writer, philosopher, educator, and patron of the arts who was born in Philadelphia, Pennsylvania, in 1885. He was the author of *The New Negro* and the first African American Rhodes scholar.

FLORENCE MILLS, born in 1896, moved to New York City around 1905 and performed in theater productions with her sisters as the Mills Sisters. In the 1920s, Mills replaced one of the leading stars in the Broadway musical *Shuffle Along*, launching her into a career in jazz and theater.

Zora Neale Hurston's MULES AND MEN is a groundbreaking collection of African American folklore that was originally published in 1935.

PAUL ROBESON, an African American actor, singer, author, political activist, and athlete, was born in Princeton, New Jersey, in 1898. He attended Rutgers University and was the valedictorian of his graduating class, after which he received a law degree from Columbia University. His popularity

as a singer and actor enabled him to fight for justice and peace in the United States and abroad.

AUGUSTA SAVAGE, a sculptor, was born in Green Cove Springs, Florida, in 1892. After studying at Cooper Union in New York City, she was turned down for an art program in France because of her race. Eventually she won a Julius Rosenwald Fellowship to study in Paris. She is known as an artist and activist who throughout her life helped many young African American artists.

SAVOY BALLROOM, located in Harlem on Lenox Avenue between West 140th Street and West 141st Street, opened in 1926. Famous musicians such as Count Basie, Benny Goodman, and Chick Webb were featured at this elegant ballroom.

The SCHOMBURG LIBRARY, now known as the Schomburg Center for Research in Black Culture, is a research unit of the New York Public Library (NYPL) located in Harlem. In 1925 it began operating as the Division of Negro Literature, History and Prints under the auspices of the NYPL. Its vast archival collections provide print and digital information about the history and culture of people of African descent.

SEVENTH AVENUE, also known as Adam Clayton Powell Jr. Boulevard, is a well-known street in Harlem, New York.

SHUFFLE ALONG, an all-black musical comedy, opened on Broadway in 1921. The show, about a mayoral election and a love story, was written by Flournoy Miller and Aubrey Lyles. It was a hit and demonstrated that African Americans play a significant role in American theater.

HENRY O. TANNER, the first African American painter to gain international acclaim, was born in Pittsburgh, Pennsylvania, in 1859. His most famous painting, *The Banjo Lesson*, is a realistic portrayal of an African American elder teaching a young boy to play the banjo.

"TUXEDO JUNCTION" is a song written in 1939 and popularized by trumpeter Erskine Hawkins and saxophonist Bill Johnson.

MADAM C. J. WALKER, born in Louisiana on December 23, 1867, is best known for her invention of African American hair care products, which led her to become the richest woman in Harlem. She developed a secret formula to stimulate hair growth and opened a beauty school in Indianapolis. She became the first self-made American female millionaire. Madam Walker died in 1919.

WELL'S RESTAURANT, founded by Joseph Wells in 1938, is best known as the restaurant that invented chicken and waffles.

CARTER G. WOODSON, an African American historian known as the Father of Black History, was born in 1875 in New Canton, Virginia. He was the second African American to receive a PhD from Harvard University. The founder of the Association for the Study of Negro Life and History in 1915, he was also the founder of Negro History Week (now Black History Month) in 1926, during the Harlem Renaissance.

FOR FURTHER READING

BLACK STARS OF THE HARLEM RENAISSANCE, edited by Jim Haskins. John Wiley & Sons: 2002.

HARLEM STOMP!: A CULTURAL HISTORY OF THE HARLEM RENAISSANCE, by Laban Carrick Hill. Little, Brown Books for Young Readers: 2009.

A HISTORY OF THE AFRICAN AMERICAN PEOPLE, edited by James Oliver Horton and Lois E. Horton. Wayne State University Press: 1997.

LANGSTON HUGHES: POET OF THE HARLEM RENAISSANCE (AFRICAN-AMERICAN BIOGRAPHIES), by Christine M. Hill. Enslow: 1997.

SHIMMY SHIMMY SHIMMY LIKE MY SISTER KATE: LOOKING AT THE HARLEM RENAISSANCE THROUGH POEMS, edited by Nikki Giovanni. Henry Holt: 1996.